The Unicorn
in the Castle

Story by Rachel McGaw • Illustrated by P.S. Brooks

Scotland's myths and legends are full
of fabled and fantastic creatures.

So much so that Scotland's national
animal is not one that you'll find in the
wild or in a zoo, on a farm or in
your house.

It's a magical and mysterious creature
that exists only in pictures and stories and
in your own imagination…

This book belongs to:

....

FORTH BOOKS

Amber and Alfie MacCaley were aged 8 and 6. Amber liked dancing and Alfie liked dressing up and playing make believe.

It was Alfie's first big school holiday and the MacCaleys were going to visit Uncle Angus. Alfie was very excited because he lived in a huge castle on top of a hill. He'd only ever seen the castle in pictures, but Alfie was sure that Uncle Angus must secretly be a king or a lord or a laird ~ or maybe even a wizard.

The road to the castle was very steep. From the bottom of the hill,
the castle looked enormous. It had a zig-zag roof
with pointy turrets and at the top of its tower
was a flag with Uncle Angus's special family
crest on it.

Alfie was thrilled. He'd brought all of his dressing up
clothes to play knights and dragons with Amber. Amber wasn't
as excited ~ she thought there was something a bit scary about the castle.
She had a funny, bubbly feeling in her tummy. But, because Alfie's smile
was so wide and happy, she didn't say anything about it.

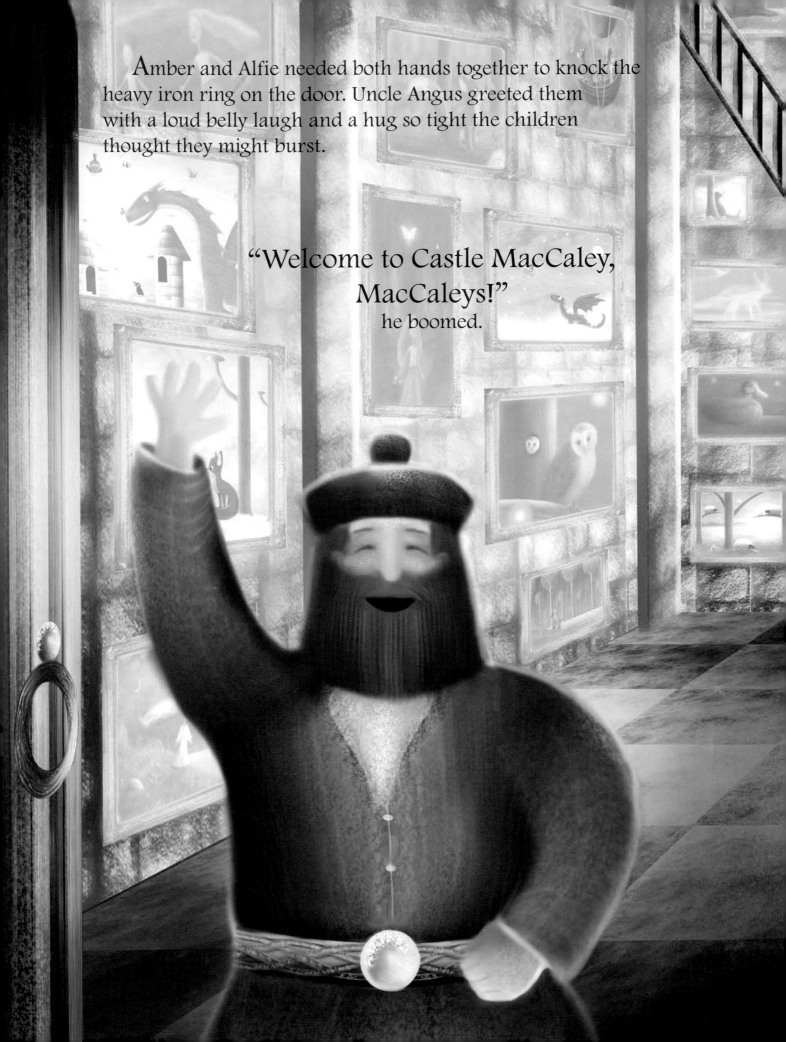

Amber and Alfie needed both hands together to knock the heavy iron ring on the door. Uncle Angus greeted them with a loud belly laugh and a hug so tight the children thought they might burst.

"Welcome to Castle MacCaley, MacCaleys!"
he boomed.

Inside, a great hall opened behind him with two wooden staircases and hundreds of paintings hanging in gold frames.

Alfie let out a squeal of excitement. This was just like the castles in his imagination when he played knights and dragons. He squeezed Amber's hand and looked up at her with round, sparkly eyes.

"Canweplay?" he said in one quick sound.

Even Amber thought that the castle was pretty special. It looked like the castles in her fairytale books with its tall windows and coloured glass.

"Okay Alfie," she said, "let's play."

At teatime, Uncle Angus called for the children to come to the dining room and they followed the swish-swash of his kilt as he walked. At the end of the hall, Alfie spotted a door. It didn't look very welcoming though.

It had metal spikes poking out and in the middle there was a thick, black cross. Amber saw it too - this door gave her the same funny feeling she had at the bottom of the hill.

Uncle Angus noticed Alfie and Amber looking at the door.

"Now, children," he said, "this is important. That door is always closed. It must always stay closed. You must promise your Uncle that you will never go through that door. There's nothing for you to find and it's not a safe place."

"If there's nothing to find," asked Amber, "why isn't it safe?"
Uncle Angus stepped closer so that he towered over the children.

"Never you mind what's in there, lass," he replied.

"Just don't go through that door."

With that, Uncle Angus spun around and opened
the doors to the dining room. Alfie gasped as the longest
table he had ever seen stretched across the room.

"There must be more than a hundred chairs!" he said.

At the end of the table, Mum and Dad were sitting so the
children ran up to join them, while Uncle Angus followed.
The MacCaleys had a lovely meal together
and then Amber and Alfie were sent to bed.

Upstairs, Amber climbed into bed and drew the thick, heavy curtains. She slept for a while and when she woke the room was dark. At first she thought she might still be dreaming, because she could hear a strange noise.

It sounded like grunting. It wasn't Alfie snoring though ~ she was used to hearing that. There was also a scraping sound and then the jangling of metal. She had that funny feeling again in her tummy.

Amber couldn't think what might make that noise. She peeked through the curtains but couldn't see much in the dark. She listened and wondered what it might be until she fell asleep again.

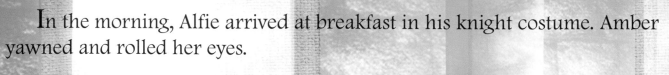

In the morning, Alfie arrived at breakfast in his knight costume. Amber yawned and rolled her eyes.

"What are you wearing that for?" she asked.

"Because I am **Sir Alfie Runsalot,** bravest knight of the realm!" he replied.

"Come and play knights with me Amber," Alfie said after breakfast.

"I don't feel like it," Amber yawned.

"I'm too tired."

Alfie asked why and Amber told him all about the strange noises she had heard from her bed.

"I know what that is!" said Alfie,
jumping around and swishing his sword.

"It's a dragon!"

"Don't be silly," said Amber,
"dragons aren't real."

"Yes they are," he replied.

"And I know where to find one,"
he said, turning on his heels.

Alfie took off at speed down the hallway. Amber followed as quickly as she could, but she just caught sight of him scoot through the door.

The door that was meant to be closed.

The door that Uncle Angus said they must not go through.

The door to wherever it was that Uncle Angus said **was not safe.**

Amber turned to find Mum and Dad, but she could hear
Uncle Angus's voice in her ears.

"You must promise not to go through that door," he had said.

Alfie had broken that promise and that meant he would be in trouble.
Amber didn't want that, so instead of finding Mum and Dad, she followed
Alfie through the door.

On the other side it was very dark. Amber crept forward and bumped into Alfie who had stopped still.

"What are you doing?" she whispered.

Alfie didn't reply. On the wall, there was a lantern. Amber lifted it and touched the flame to a candle, and one after another dozens of candles lit all around the room.

In the flickering light, Amber could see what had stopped Alfie in his tracks. Across the room was a strange creature. It looked a bit like a horse, and a bit like a dragon, but not much like anything the children had ever seen before. It was pure white, with long legs and a long face, and an enormous pointed horn on the top of its head.

"Alfie..." said Amber, "that's not a dragon."

Alfie looked up at her with frightened eyes and nodded.

Amber's voice stirred the creature. As it moved, Amber heard again the jangling of metal - just like the night before when she heard the noise in her bedroom. She saw that the noise came from long, thick, gold chains that wrapped around the creature's body and locked it to the fireplace at the end of the room.

Standing tall, the creature let out a grunt and clouds of breath puffed from its nostrils. It scratched its feet against the stone floor and dust rose all around. It reared up on its back legs and shook its head, its bright, white mane glistening in the candlelight.

Alfie was terrified and grabbed Amber's hand. "It's gonna get us!" he shouted.

"We need to go!"

The children ran back through the door and shut it tight with shaking hands.

"What was that?" asked Alfie.

"I don't know," Amber replied, "but I think I've seen it before."
She led Alfie back into the dining room. In the daylight
they could see that the walls were covered by three
enormous tapestries.

The first tapestry showed the creature in
a beautiful garden surrounded by people.
The garden looked just like Uncle Angus's
garden at the Castle.

In the second tapestry the creature was captured inside a tall, round fence. It lay on the ground with its head down. In the last tapestry, the creature was tied down and covered in gold chains.

Above the tapestries hung a long banner with writing. Alfie tried his best to read it.

"Cuh-ah-leh-eh..."

"C-a-l-e-d-o-n-i-a-n"

"Caledonian," he announced, proudly.

The second word was a bit harder. "Uh ~ uhn ~ uhni… onion?" he asked himself.

"I can't read this word," he said.

Amber looked up.

"Caledonian Unicorn," she said.

The children looked at each other. Neither knew what that might be, or why it would be locked up inside Uncle Angus's castle.

Alfie said that they should tell Mum and Dad because it must be a dangerous thing to be chained to the fireplace. But Amber reminded him that they had broken their promise and that they would be in trouble.

That night, Amber lay awake and thought about the unicorn. She couldn't understand why Uncle Angus would keep it locked up in the dark. Earlier, Amber had looked right into the unicorn's eyes. Through the dust clouds, Amber didn't see anger or danger in its eyes.

She saw sadness. And hope.

The next morning, Amber whispered to Alfie that she was going to go to see the unicorn. He looked at her wide-eyed.

"You can't, Amber, it might hurt you!" he said.
She explained that she didn't think it was fair that it was locked up. She wondered when it had last seen daylight or been shown any kindness.

Alfie said that if she was going, then he would go with her. He rushed upstairs and emerged dressed again as Sir Alfie Runsalot.

"If it comes for you, I'll protect you,"

he declared.

When no one was looking, the children slipped through the door again.

"Just wait here, Alfie," said Amber, taking the lantern.

The unicorn's chains rattled as it stood up.

Alfie waited near the door. As he looked up, he noticed that there was another tapestry on the wall of this room. It showed the unicorn unchained, being led through a garden by a girl in a white dress.

Suddenly, Alfie heard a clatter and Amber let out a shriek as she tripped and fell, scraping her knees and burning her fingers. At the sound of Amber's cry, the unicorn reared on its back legs. Alfie ran as fast as he could to help his sister.

The unicorn strained against the metal chains with all its might towards the children. Alfie was terrified it was going to hurt them, just as he thought. He knelt, trembling, pointed his sword toward the unicorn and covered Amber with his shield.

The unicorn towered over the children and leaned forward. Both were frightened and had tears in their eyes.

They gripped each other tightly.

And then, to Alfie's surprise, the unicorn delicately touched the top of Amber's head with the very tip of its horn.

A flash of light **burst** across the room.

When it dimmed, everything was quiet. Amber had stopped crying and looked at her hand ~ there was no sign of a burn. She looked at her knees and there were no scrapes and no scratches.

Amber rose and slowly walked towards the unicorn. It stood still, the chains pressed against its body. She reached out and touched its neck, and in return it gently nuzzled the top of her head.

"You healed me," she said.

Suddenly, the door to the hall burst open and Uncle Angus appeared.

"Children!" he shouted, "get away from that beast!" Uncle Angus pulled at the unicorn's chains.

The unicorn reared and grunted and stamped its feet.

"Get away, children!" Uncle Angus repeated.

"No, Uncle Angus!" shouted Amber. "Let it go!"

"This is a dangerous beast," he yelled.

"It's not," cried Amber.
She ran across and stood right between Uncle Angus and the unicorn.

"It healed me when I fell," she said, pointing to her hand.
"Alfie saw too," she said.

Uncle Angus looked at Alfie who nodded his head.

"It's true ~ I did," he said.

"There was a really big flash and then like magic
she was all better."

Uncle Angus loosened his grip on the chains and
the unicorn stood down. Amber stroked its neck
and it nuzzled her again.

"You see," she said,
"it's a gentle creature."

Uncle Angus was baffled.

"This beast has been held captive by the MacCaleys for generations. You've seen the tapestries upstairs. In all folklore it is known to be the most dangerous beast when free and so it must be chained by the MacCaley family for our protection," he said.

"But what about that one?" asked Alfie, tugging on his Uncle's kilt. He pointed to the tapestry of the unicorn and the girl.

"That was stitched by Lady Jennie MacCaley a hundred years ago," he said.

"She said that the beast could be tamed by a fair maiden, but no one believed her."

Uncle Angus and Alfie looked at Amber, who was gently stroking the unicorn's mane.

"Perhaps she was right," Uncle Angus said.

Together the children and Uncle Angus released the unicorn from its chains. It didn't rear or run, or scrape its feet.

Instead it trotted alongside Amber through the door and out into the castle gardens.

Uncle Angus, Mum and Dad watched the children playing in the garden. They spoke about Amber's power to tame the unicorn and decided that it would be best to stay at Castle MacCaley so that the unicorn could be free.

The children were delighted ~ it would be just like living in a fairy tale. Alfie could be a proper knight and Amber would have the unicorn to play with every day.

From then on, the family lived happily together in the castle. The unicorn was free to roam the gardens and would never be chained again.

And no one was ever sick or ever hurt,
because the unicorn took care of
the MacCaley family forever.

The End

Where might you find a unicorn, reader?

When you next visit an ancient castle, beautiful garden or historic house, close your eyes and try to imagine your very own rare Scottish unicorn.

If you're very good at imagining, a unicorn might even visit you at home…

FORTH BOOKS

First Published 2019 by Forth Books

www.forthbooks.co.uk

Text © Rachel McGaw

Illustrations © P.S. Brooks

ISBN 978-1-909266-20-9

Printed in China